ROOOOARR

Louis the Tiger Who Came From the Sea

MICHAL KOZLOWSKI

ART BY
SHOLTO WALKER

annick press
toronto + new york + vancouver

Early one summer morning,
just as the birds were stretching their wings
and practicing their songs,

Ali and Ollie were woken by a **beastly** snore coming from the yard.

When they looked out the window,
Ali had to rub her eyes
because she thought she had seen
a giant carrot in the grass.

Then Ollie had to rub his eyes
because he thought he had seen
a huge pumpkin in the grass.

And when they had rubbed their eyes enough,
they saw that it was a tiger snoring in the yard.

He was soaking wet, and in his sleep he rolled back
and forth as if he were dreaming of dolphins in the surf.

"How did
he get here?"
asked Ollie.

"He looks
like he came
from the sea,"
said Ali.

And so they opened the window and could smell fish and saltwater.

Now they were sure the tiger had come from the sea.

"What do you think his name is?" asked Ollie.

"He looks like a tiger
named **Louis** to me,"
said Ali.

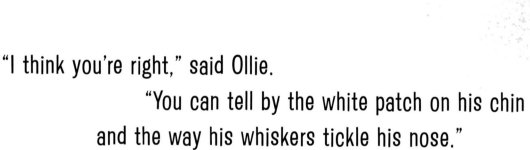

"I think you're right," said Ollie.
"You can tell by the white patch on his chin
and the way his whiskers tickle his nose."

"And what do you do
with tigers named Louis
who come from the sea?"
asked Ollie.

"I think you feed them," said Ali.

So Ali and Ollie
climbed down the stairs
and got the
biggest bucket
they could find.

They filled it with
one jug of milk,
    and then another,
    and then a box of cereal
and took it into
    the yard for Louis.

His snores made **waves** in the bucket so the milk looked just like an angry, white ocean.

Then Mother and Father, who had been sleeping all this time,
came into the yard to see what Ali and Ollie were doing.

Just then, Louis awoke
and let out a great big

ROOOOOAAR

and everyone ran inside.

RRRRRRRRRRRRRRRRRRRRRRRRR

They were so scared they forgot to close the door.
So when Louis finished eating his cereal,
he just walked into the house
through the open door

and lay down in front
of the fireplace
and went back to sleep.

But Mother and Father had never heard of a tiger coming from the sea and they did not believe that Louis came from there.

All that day, Louis the tiger slept in front of the fireplace and
Ali and Ollie and Mother and Father had to stay upstairs so they did not wake him.

In the evening,
Mother ran the bath
for Ollie.

But when Ollie came into the bathroom, Louis was rolling around in the bathtub. So Ollie went to bed without his bath, and Mother was convinced that Louis really had come from the sea.

All that night,
Ali and Ollie lay awake,
thinking of how they
could help Louis get back
to the sea.

Ollie said they could drive Louis in the car, but he had never seen
a tiger in a car, and there was probably a good reason for that.

Ali said they could show Louis a map and point him to the sea, which was not far at all, but she had never seen a tiger read a map.

"What if we
lead him to the sea?"
asked Ollie.

"Yes," said Ali,
"if we dress up
like fishes and
sea creatures and
walk to the ocean,
he would surely
follow us."

All the next morning, Ali and Ollie gathered
materials that Mother and Father could use
to sew fish costumes. Ollie was a narwhal,
with a big tusk on his head.
Ali was a dolphin, with a long snout.

Mother was a **blowfish**, with a funny mouth,

and Father was an **octopus** with six tentacles, because there was not enough material to make eight tentacles.

So when the narwhal and the dolphin and the blowfish
and the octopus with six tentacles marched down the stairs,
Louis did not roar
when he saw them.
He leaped into
the air.

Then he followed the four
sea creatures out the door
and down the street

and through the park

and onto the beach.

Louis waded into the water and began to swim,

and swim,

and swim.

Ali and Ollie watched him until they could not tell whether it was
an orange wave or an orange Louis swimming away, because the sun had begun
to set and was casting an orange glow over the whole ocean.

Annick Press Ltd.

Cover and interior design by Irvin Cheung / iCheung Design, inc.

We acknowledge the support of the Canada Council for the Arts, the Ontario Arts Council,
and the Government of Canada through the Book Publishing Industry Development
Program (BPIDP) for our publishing activities.

ONTARIO ARTS COUNCIL
CONSEIL DES ARTS DE L'ONTARIO

Cataloging in Publication
Kozlowski, Michal
    Louis the tiger who came from the sea / Michal Kozlowski ; art by Sholto Walker.

ISBN 978-1-55451-257-7 (bound).—ISBN 978-1-55451-256-0 (pbk.)

    I. Walker, Sholto II. Title.

PS8621.O9785L68 2011   jC813'.6"   C2010-906878-5

Printed and bound in China

Published in the U.S.A. by	**Distributed in Canada by**	**Distributed in the U.S.A. by**
Annick Press (U.S.) Ltd.	Firefly Books Ltd.	Firefly Books (U.S.) Inc.
	66 Leek Crescent	P.O. Box 1338
	Richmond Hill, ON	Ellicott Station
	L4B 1H1	Buffalo, NY 14205

Visit Annick at **www.annickpress.com**

Visit Sholto Walker at **www.illustrationweb.com/SholtoWalker/**

For T.K. and J.R.-K.
—M.K.

To my son, Louis, my other tiger
—S.W.